The Secret Kitten

The Secret Kitten

by Holly Webb
Illustrated by Sophy Williams

For Poppy and Star, my not-so-secret kittens...

tiger tales

5 River Road, Suite 128, Wilton, CT 06897
Published in the United States 2017
Originally published in Great Britain 2015
by Little Tiger Press
Text copyright © 2015 Holly Webb
Illustrations copyright © 2015 Sophy Williams
Author photograph copyright © Nigel Bird
My Naughty Little Puppy illustration copyright © Kate Pankhurst
ISBN-13: 978-1-68010-400-4
ISBN-10: 1-68010-400-4
Printed in China
STP/1800/0118/0816
10 9 8 7 6 5 4 3 2 1

For more insight and activities, visit us at www.tigertalesbooks.com

Chapter One

Alicia stood on tiptoe with her elbows balanced on the windowsill, leaning out to look down at the yard. She had never had a room like this before, right up at the very top of the house. She was so high up that the yard looked strange and far below, the trees short and stubby, even though she knew that they were tall.

Actually, she had never had a room of her own before. She had always shared with Will, her little brother. But now that they were living at Grandma's house, there was space for each of them to have their own room. It was nice and really odd at the same time.

Alicia had mixed feelings about everything at the moment. Grandma's house was beautiful with a big yard, not like the tiny yard she'd had back home, but she couldn't stop thinking about the old house. They had been to Grandma's lots of times, of course, but always as visitors. Living there was going to be strange and different. The house didn't feel like it was their home yet, even though Dad had explained that he'd bought half of it from Grandma. They were all going to share. Grandma would help take care of Alicia and Will, and Dad would take care of the wild, overgrown yard that had gotten to be too much for Grandma recently, and they would all be company for each other.

It will be good for Dad, Alicia thought, resting her chin on her hands as she stared down at the trees. For the last five years, ever since their mom had died, he'd taken care of Will and her by himself. He'd had a little help from babysitters, but mostly he had been in charge of everything. Now he would have Grandma to help and maybe he wouldn't be so worried all the time. It was hard when he had to stay late at work and missed picking up Alicia and Will from after-school clubs, or the babysitter's, or their friends' houses.

Alicia swallowed hard. They wouldn't be going back to their after-school clubs. They weren't even going back to their old school—Grandma's house was too far away. On Monday, she and Will would be starting all over again at a new school.

Alicia wasn't looking forward to it.

"It'll be all right," Alicia whispered to herself. "It was nice when we went to see it." The teacher had been friendly and kind, Will had loved the big jungle gym on the playground, and it was only a five-minute walk from Grandma's house. But it was new and different, and even though there would be a coat hook ready with her name on it and a desk for her books in the classroom, Alicia knew she didn't really belong there, not yet.

Something stirred among the trees. Alicia squinted sideways, trying to figure out what it was. A bird? Then she smiled. A large orange cat was walking carefully along the fence, padding from paw to paw, slowly and deliberately. *He must belong next door*, Alicia thought.

Grandma didn't have a cat. She didn't have any pets, even though this would be the perfect house for one with its beautiful big yard. Alicia thought Grandma's neat living room would look a lot nicer with a cat draped along the back of the sofa, or curled up on the rug.

But Dad had told them that Grandma didn't like pets. She thought they were too messy and were a lot of work. Alicia wished she could argue with Grandma and say what about purring and how a cat could keep your feet warm on a cold night? But you couldn't start that kind of argument with your grandma—not her grandma, anyway. She wasn't an arguing kind of person. Alicia loved her, but Grandma was one of those people who knew she was always right. And she was the one who would be doing most of the cleaning up, too!

"Alicia!"

It was Will! Alicia spun around, hearing the wobbly, tearful note in his voice. "What's the matter?" she asked worriedly.

"Grandma yelled at me," Will sniffed. He sat down on the floor, leaning against Alicia's bed. His face was flushed, and he brushed away a tear with his hand.

"Why?" Alicia sat next to him and put her arm around his shoulders.

Will snuggled into her. "I was playing soccer in the yard and then I brought the ball back in with me and I bounced it…."

"Oh, Will! Where?" Alicia demanded and he edged away from her a little, hunching his shoulders up.

"In the living room."

"You didn't break anything, did you?" Alicia asked anxiously. Dad had made them promise to be careful, but Will was only six and sometimes he just forgot things like that.

"No!" Will protested indignantly. "But Grandma was still really angry. She said I wasn't supposed to kick balls around in the house, but I hadn't even kicked it! I was just bouncing it." He sighed and leaned back on her shoulder again, peering around Alicia's room at the cardboard boxes, already almost all unpacked.

"Do you like having your own bedroom?" he whispered seriously.

Alicia nodded. "Yes…. But last night I missed hearing you talking to your toys," she added to make him feel better.

"I do like my bedroom." Will didn't sound so sure. "But do you think I could keep all my things in my room, then sleep up here with you? I could bring my sleeping bag."

"Maybe sometimes," Alicia said comfortingly. It had been strange going to bed last night without Will snoring and snuffling on the other side of the room, but she was glad to have a place that was just her own.

All her own, except that it would be so nice to share it with a cat. *Any cat*, Alicia thought, wondering if the big orange cat from next door ever came to visit.

Chapter Two

The black-and-white kitten peered around the pile of old boxes. Her ears were laid back flat and her tail was twitching. Out in the alley between the bakery and newsstand, she could see her brother and sister playing around, chasing each other and wrestling. Her paws itched to join in. She stepped out a little further.

Then a car roared past on the main road and she darted back into her hiding place in the storage yard. Seconds later, her tabby brother and sister shot back in after her and they all huddled together in the dark little corner, hissing at the strange, frightening noise. The two tabby kittens wriggled and stamped their paws inside a broken wooden crate, making themselves comfy on the old rags and torn-up papers, trying to find the warmest, driest spot. The black-and-white kitten licked them

both lovingly, hoping that they'd all curl up together and snooze, as they waited for their mother to come back from her foraging. But the tabby kittens didn't want to hide for long. A minute or so later they were already nosing out into the alley again.

Their little sister watched them anxiously, wondering about that loud noise and hoping that whatever it was wouldn't come back. The alley was so open—she liked places where she could hide and still see everything. All that space made her nervous.

"Oh, look! Kittens!"

A little boy came running into the alley and the tabby kittens streaked back toward the old boxes, knocking their black-and-white sister sideways. She huddled at the back of their little den, her heart thumping, but the bravest of the tabbies was too curious to stay hidden, even with the boy blundering around, his feet stamping and thudding. She scrambled out past the broken board onto the top of the box and gazed at him.

"Mom, look...," the little boy whispered. "It really is a kitten! She's tiny!"

"Isn't she? She's beautiful."

The black-and-white kitten squeaked worriedly. There was someone else out there, too. She wished her sister would come back, but now her brother was wriggling out to see what was going on.

"Oh, there's two! Look, Owen, the other one came out to see you. I wonder who they belong to! I guess they're strays, but they look very young. Their mother must be around somewhere."

The voices were soft and gentle, and the black-and-white kitten stretched her paws, shook her whiskers, and began to creep toward the opening. Maybe she would go and see what was happening….

But then the little boy shrieked with laughter as kitten whiskers tickled his fingers. The kitten ran back and buried herself in the rags again. At last she heard their footsteps echoing back down the alleyway and she relaxed a bit. Then a tabby-striped face pushed in through the gap between the boxes and she darted forward to nuzzle happily at her mother. The thin tabby cat had been hiding out of the way until the little boy and his mom were gone. She had always been a stray and she wasn't very fond of people. People meant food, but sometimes they threw things and shouted at her for pawing around in garbage cans. She avoided them as much as she could.

The tabby kittens piled in after her and tore at the ham sandwich she'd found for them, scrambling and hissing over the delicious pieces of ham. The kittens were eight weeks old and they were all still drinking her milk as well as eating food, but they were always hungry.

The black-and-white kitten finished her piece of sandwich and snuggled up against her mother. She was warm and safe and full of food. Her brother and sister flopped down on top of her in a softly purring pile of fur, and all four of them curled up to sleep.

"So, how was it?" Grandma asked, smiling at Alicia as they walked home from school on Monday. She didn't need to ask how school had been for Will. He was bouncing around the pavement in front of them with his new best friend, Henry, doing ninja kicks.

"It was okay," Alicia said, not very enthusiastically. It was true. No one had been mean and she'd understood the work they were doing. Emma, the girl who'd been told to give her a hand, had been nice and had made sure she knew where everything was.

But she'd stayed on the sidelines of all the games. And everyone knew secret jokes about the teachers that she didn't and there was no one who knew all the fun things about her, the things her friends back home knew. She was just a boring new girl.

Grandma put an arm around her shoulders. "It'll get better, Alicia, I promise. In a month, it won't feel like a new school anymore."

Alicia blinked. She hadn't expected Grandma to notice that she wasn't really happy. "I guess so," she mumbled and smiled gratefully at Grandma.

"Why don't we stop in at the bakery and get a treat? To celebrate school being just about all right?" Grandma suggested.

Will turned around mid-air and came racing back to them, saying good-bye to Henry. "Cupcakes? Can we? Can I have a marshmallow cream one?"

Grandma made a face. "I guess so. I don't know how you can eat those things, though."

"It's really easy," Will told her solemnly and Alicia giggled, feeling the nervous lump inside her melt away for the first time that day.

It was as they were coming out of the bakery, each clutching a rustling paper bag, that Alicia first saw the kittens. She wondered afterward if they'd heard the bags crinkling, and were hoping that she and Will might drop some food.

She'd seen a flash out of the corner of her eye, a darting movement in the alley. Alicia almost didn't stop to look at first—she'd thought that it was probably just pigeons, hopping around and looking for crumbs—but then something had made her turn back and look more closely.

The soft gray shadows peering out from behind the garbage cans had been cats!

No, kittens. Tiny kittens, two of them, their green eyes round and huge in little striped faces.

Alicia reached out her hand to grab Will, who was explaining very seriously to Grandma that it was important to eat a marshmallow cream cupcake from the bottom up, because then you got to save the marshmallow for last.

"Ow! What?"

"Look…," Alicia whispered, pulling him closer so that he'd see. "But shhh!"

"What am I looking at and you didn't have to grab me, Alicia, Dad says—Oh!"

Grandma peered over their heads. "Please tell me that's not a rat."

"They're kittens, Grandma. Can we go and take a closer look? Please?"

Grandma looked at the shops on either side of the alley. "Well, I don't think they'll mind. Don't go into the yard, though, and don't touch them."

Alicia and Will crept down the alley, holding hands. The little tabby kittens stared at them from behind the garbage cans. They were crouched low to the ground, ready to spring away to safety, but they stayed still as the children came closer.

When they were almost at the garbage cans, Alicia knelt down, gently pulling Will with her.

"Can't we go closer?" he begged.

"Not yet," she whispered back. "When I went to Jenny's house, her cat was really shy and I had to sit like this for a while, but then he climbed into my lap and let me cuddle him. Jenny says he never does that." Suddenly, Alicia was blinking away tears, thinking of Jenny and all her friends back home.

"They're coming closer." Will poked her arm impatiently. "Look!"

Alicia dragged her hand across her eyes. It was true—one of the kittens had padded all the way out now—and he was almost close enough to sniff at Will's outstretched fingers.

Then, suddenly, he darted forward and dabbed his nose at Will's hand.

Will squeaked delightedly. "His nose is all cold and damp!"

The kitten disappeared back behind the garbage cans in a blur.

"I'm sorry!" Will whispered.

But it only took seconds for the kitten to be brave enough to peek out again, and this time the other tabby kitten followed him, sniffing curiously at Alicia's school shoes.

Very slowly, Alicia reached out and petted the kitten's striped head with the tips of her fingers—the fur was so soft, almost silky. And then the kitten purred, so loudly that Alicia couldn't help giggling. The noise seemed too big for such a tiny creature.

"I wonder where their mother is," Alicia whispered to Will, looking down the alley to see if the mother cat was watching them playing with her babies.

"Are they lost?" Will asked worriedly.

"No," Grandma said quietly behind them. "I was just talking to Emma, the girl from the bakery. She said that they live in the yard—there's a pile of old boxes and things. She's been putting some food out for them."

"They live in a box?" Alicia said, thinking how cold it had been the night before.

Grandma nodded. "Yes. But apparently a couple of her regular customers are thinking of trying to adopt these two, once they're big enough to leave their mother. That won't be long."

"Grandma, there's another one!" Alicia gasped. "I was looking for their mom, but there's a kitten peeking out of that old box! A black-and-white one!"

"Yes, there is!" Grandma looked over to where Alicia was pointing. "That's odd. The girl in the bakery only mentioned the two tabbies. Maybe that little one isn't as friendly as the others. I'm sorry, you two, but we have to get going. I need to get dinner ready." She smiled down at Alicia's disappointed face. "I'm sure they'll still be here tomorrow...."

Chapter Three

They were late the next morning because Will had spilled half a bowl of cereal on his school uniform, so there was no time to stop and play with kittens. Alicia looked down the alley hopefully on their way to school, but she couldn't see even a whisker. She imagined all the kittens sleeping in, curled up snugly in their old box.

When they stopped on the way home, Emma, the lady from the bakery, was there, putting some trash out in the garbage cans. She smiled at Alicia and Will and said, "Are you looking for those kittens? I'm really sorry, but that lady I was telling your grandmother about came and took them home with her this morning."

"Oh...." Alicia swallowed. Will's eyes had filled with tears and she felt like crying, too. She nudged her little brother. "That's good," she said firmly, trying to convince herself as well as Will. "It's getting colder now that it's fall. Imagine sleeping outside in a box all winter."

Grandma nodded. "It would be horrible. Damp and chilly. They're much better off with a nice home inside."

"I know." Will sniffed. "But I wanted to see them. We only got to see them once."

"I'll miss them," Emma said, as Alicia and Will turned to go. "Cute little pair. Beautiful stripes."

Alicia glanced back at her. "But— there was a black-and-white kitten, too. Did she take all three of them?"

Emma blinked. "Three? Really? I thought there were only two of them."

"No." Alicia shook her head. "Definitely three. We saw the black-and-white one yesterday."

"She's right," Grandma put in. "I saw her, too. She reminded me of the cat I had when I was a little girl. She was named Catkin. This kitten had the same pretty white tip on her tail."

Alicia glanced at Will in surprise. Grandma had had a cat of her own? Dad had said she didn't like pets.

Will wasn't really listening, though. "Grandma, is the little kitten left all on her own now?"

"Her mom's still there," Emma pointed out.

"No other kittens to play with, though," Alicia said sadly.

Will beamed at her. "Maybe she'll come and play with us instead, then, if she's lonely." He ran a few steps further down the alley and called, "Here, kitty, kitty!"

"She won't come out if you yell at her," Alicia said. "We've got to be gentle. Maybe tempt her out. Could we buy some cat treats, Grandma?"

"I suppose." Grandma nodded. "Maybe if that kitten gets more used to people, someone will take her home, too."

Alicia caught her breath. She almost asked Grandma if they could be the ones to give the kitten a home. But then she remembered everything Dad had said about having to keep the house neat and not damaging Grandma's things and how Grandma hated messes. And then she thought about Jenny's mom rolling her eyes and sighing and saying, "Oh, not again!" when Jenny's cat, Socks, had knocked a vase of flowers off the kitchen table.

There was no way Grandma would let them have a cat, even if the kitten did look like her old pet, Catkin.

Alicia frowned down at her magazine. It was her favorite one, a pet magazine that she got every week. She'd brought it into school to read at recess. Everyone was still being friendly, but she hated having to ask to join in the games. It was embarrassing. It was easier to sit on one of the benches and read.

This week's magazine had a big article on animal charities and an interview with the manager of an ASPCA shelter. She was talking about how important it was to find cats new homes quickly, as they didn't really like being kept all together. They wanted a place to call their own. Alicia sighed to herself as she thought of the black-and-white kitten.

But the really strange thing was that the ASPCA lady also said that black cats and black-and-white ones were much harder to find homes for than tabbies or orange tigers. Alicia just couldn't understand why. The article said that people thought black-and-white cats were too ordinary, not pretty like tabbies.

It made Alicia so angry that she almost tore the page because she was gripping it so tightly. How could people think that? All cats and kittens were different! Jenny's cat Socks was white, with an orange tail and a funny orange stripe down his nose. But that didn't mean he was a better pet than the little black-and-white kitten would be.

The article also said that some people didn't want cats that were black all over because they were worried that they might not be seen on the road and could get run over. *At least that makes sense*, Alicia thought. But they could always get their black cat a reflective collar, couldn't they?

"If I ever get a cat, I'm definitely going to a shelter and choosing a black-and-white one," she said. "Or a pretty black cat. Like a witch's cat."

"Is it good?"

Alicia jumped so hard she almost banged her head on the back of the bench, and the girl leaning over to talk to her gasped.

"I'm sorry! I didn't mean to scare you. I get that magazine sometimes, too. I was just wondering if it was a good one this week."

"Oh!" Alicia nodded and smiled. "Yes. But kind of sad. There's a big article about shelters. And it says not many people choose the black cats. I was just thinking I definitely would."

"Oh, me, too," the other girl agreed.

Alicia thought frantically, trying to remember her name. There were a lot of girls in her class, but she thought this one was named Sarah. "Our cat's mostly black, but he has a white front and white paws. My mom says he looks like he's wearing a penguin suit." She leaned over and looked at the article. "What's that about Black Cat Appreciation Day?"

Alicia looked at the bubble down near the bottom of the page. "It's to show everyone that black cats are special. It's in August here but it says in England it's in October—oh, the same day as Halloween. I guess that makes sense. But black cats aren't all spooky."

Sarah giggled. "They're good at appearing out of nowhere, though. I'm always tripping over Harvey."

"Aw, that's such a cute name for a cat." Alicia smiled.

"He just looks like a Harvey," Sarah explained. "Even when he was a kitten, there was something Harvey-ish about him. Do you have a cat?" she added, looking at Alicia sideways. There was something hopeful about the way she asked it, as though she wanted someone to share cat stories with. A friend who had a cat of her own—what could be better than that?

It was the first time someone had really seemed interested in her at school. If she said no, Sarah would shrug and smile and walk away, Alicia was sure of it. And she was just as sure that she didn't want that to happen. So she nodded, slowly, trying to think about what to say. "Yes. We have a kitten." She slipped her hand under the magazine and crossed her fingers. She hated to lie, especially to someone as nice as Sarah, but she had to. "We just got her." It was almost true, wasn't it? She wanted that little black-and-white kitten from the alley to be theirs, so much....

"Oh, you're so lucky! Is she pretty? What does she look like? How old is she?"

Alicia swallowed. "She's black-and-white, like Harvey. And she's very little, just old enough to leave her mother. She was a stray."

"What's her name?" Sarah demanded eagerly.

Alicia blinked. She couldn't think. Not a single name would come into her head. What was a good name for a kitten?

Then she smiled at Sarah. She knew the perfect name.

"Her name is Catkin."

Chapter Four

"What's the matter, Alicia?" Grandma looked up from her book and peered across the table at her granddaughter's pile of books. "You haven't written anything in a while."

"It's a project." Alicia sighed. "It's hard. It's about Egyptians and we can make the project about whatever we want—that's what's so hard about it.

I can't choose, even though I've got all these books from the library."

And, of course, only half her mind was on her project. The rest of it was worrying about having lied to Sarah two days ago. Especially since Sarah was really, really excited. She kept asking about Catkin, and she obviously really wanted to come and see her. But she was too nice—or maybe too shy—to come right out and ask if she could come over. Alicia had a feeling that she was working herself up to it, though.

The awful thing was, Alicia would have liked Sarah to come over. She'd love to have a friend come over to play. Grandma and Dad kept gently asking if there was anyone she really liked at school and if she wanted to invite somebody over. Will had had Henry come over and had been over to his house, too. And he'd been invited to a birthday party already.

But if Sarah came over, she'd know that Alicia had been lying about Catkin and she'd hate her. She might even tell the entire class that Alicia was a liar.

"I went to Egypt, you know," Grandma said thoughtfully, breaking into Alicia's thoughts. "It must have been, oh, goodness, eight, ten years ago? Yes, just before you were born, Alicia. I went to see the pyramids with one of my friends from school, Aunt Barbara. Do you remember her?"

Alicia didn't, but she nodded as if she did. "You really went there? What was it like? Did you go and see the Great Pyramid?"

"We certainly did. We went inside it, too. It was pretty scary," Grandma added slowly. "Very shadowy, and it was hard to breathe. I have to admit that I didn't like it much, Alicia, but I'm glad I saw it. And from the outside, the pyramids were incredible to look at. Wait a minute." She smiled and got up, walking into the living room. Alicia could hear her opening drawers in the big display cabinet that had most of her precious, breakable possessions in it.

Grandma came back in, carefully unrolling a piece of brownish paper. "This is what I brought back as a souvenir of the vacation, Alicia. It's a papyrus. Like paper, but made out of reeds." She held it out. "You can take a look."

Alicia looked at her uncertainly. "Isn't it fragile?" she asked worriedly. She wanted to hold it—she could see that the painting on it was beautiful, a black cat wearing a jeweled necklace and even an earring, it looked like.

"I know you'll be careful." Grandma smiled at her. "I should get it framed, really. It's such a beautiful painting. The box on the side says my name in hieroglyphics. I watched the man doing it."

Alicia took the papyrus, feeling the roughness against her fingers. She could even see the lines of the reed stems in the weave. "The cat's so beautiful," she said. Then she grinned up at Grandma. "I can't see many cats agreeing to wear all that jewelry, though. Most of them don't even like collars!"

Grandma nodded. "But this one is a goddess. Her name is Bast."

Alicia examined the picture again. "There was a cat goddess? Wow…. Grandma, I could do my project on her!" Very carefully, she laid the papyrus down on the table so she could fling her arms around her grandmother.

"Maybe I could even copy the painting!"

As she hugged Grandma tightly, Alicia realized something else. Grandma couldn't possibly dislike cats that much, could she? Not when she'd chosen a painting of a cat as a special souvenir.

The black-and-white kitten was enjoying a patch of sunlight in the yard. Her mother was off looking for food and the little kitten was stretched out, snoozing, with her nose on her paws.

Her ears fluttered a little as she heard a noise, coming from the back of one of the shops, and then her eyes flew open. Someone was coming!

She darted back into the safety of the box, her heart thudding fast against her ribs. The voices were loud, frightening even, and there were heavy feet clumping all around her.

She pressed herself back into the corner of the box, thinking that they would just dump their garbage in the cans and go. But no one usually came close to the pile of old boxes like this. It wasn't a delivery—no van had driven down the alley. She was almost used to that noise, although she still didn't like it.

This was something different. And then suddenly the box, her safe, warm box, shifted and split and she let out a high-pitched squeak of fright. What was happening?

"There's something in there," a deep voice growled. "Ugh, not rats, I hope."

"I don't think so—there's a stray cat that hangs around the yard. Maybe it's her."

Someone clapped his hands loudly, the sound sharp and echoing in the enclosed yard. "Go on, shoo! Get lost, cat!"

The kitten squeaked again and her box tipped sideways. She shot out, terrified, and streaked across the yard, away from the growling voices.

"There she goes—but that's just a kitten. Not much bigger than a rat, poor little thing!"

The kitten huddled in the corner, panicking. Someone was coming toward her, huge boots thumping. She had never tried to climb the fences before, but anything was better than staying here. She sank her claws in the wood and scrambled frantically upward, balancing for a moment on the very top of the fence. Then she jumped down the other side and set off through the bushes, to who knew where.

Alicia was stretched out in the long grass, idly picking the blades. She'd done her homework and typed up a lot of work for her project on the computer. She felt relaxed and happy in the autumn sun. Grandma had given her a sandwich to keep her going until Dad got home and they could all have dinner together, but Alicia hadn't finished it—she was feeling too lazy even to eat.

She could hear Will at the end of the yard, humming to himself as he investigated the greenhouse. Grandma didn't use it very much these days and some of the glass panes were broken, but Dad had told them he'd plant seeds in the springtime. He'd already cleaned up part of the yard closest to the house, but Alicia and Will loved this wild part, with the overgrown bushes. It was full of hidden nests and little dark caves. Alicia glanced sideways, checking that the big spotted garden spider hanging off the branch by her foot hadn't moved. She didn't mind him being there—he'd probably lived here longer than she had—but she didn't want him getting any closer.

He was still there. But underneath him, peering out at her from the shadows, was a tiny black-and-white face.

A kitten! The same kitten she had seen in the alleyway, Alicia was almost sure. She looked across the yard at the greenhouse and the fence. She hadn't realized before, but the shops were very close to Grandma's backyard, even though to get to them by the street you had to go a long way around.

"Did you climb over the fence?" Alicia whispered, very, very quietly.

The kitten stared back at her. *She's so small and thin*, Alicia thought. She looked exhausted—as though she was frightened, but too worn out even to run.

Slowly, creeping her fingers across the grass, Alicia stretched out a hand to get her sandwich. It was chicken. Perfect for a kitten treat.

The kitten watched her, wide-eyed, shrinking back a little as Alicia's hand came close. But then she smelled the chicken—Alicia could see the exact moment. Her whiskers twitched and her ears flicked forward, then her eyes grew even rounder.

Alicia tore off a tiny piece of sandwich and gently laid it down, just where the tufts of long grass met the branches.

Then she watched. The kitten didn't have to move far. If she wasn't brave enough, maybe Alicia could throw her a piece further in, but that might scare her away.

The kitten looked at the piece of sandwich, and Alicia could see her sniffing. She looked between Alicia and the sandwich a few times, then she wriggled forward on her stomach, inching slowly toward the food. As soon as she was close enough, she seized the yummy mouthful and darted back into the safety of the bush.

Alicia wanted to laugh, but she folded her lips together firmly, in case the noise scared the kitten away. She watched the kitten wolf down the scrap and then she tore off a little more. This time she left it a little closer to her feet.

The kitten didn't take as long to decide if she was going for the food the second time. She gave Alicia one slightly suspicious look and then raced to grab it.

After that, Alicia put the plate down, right next to her feet, to see what would happen. Surely the kitten wouldn't be able to drag away a whole sandwich, would she? She'd have to stop by the plate and eat it there. And then maybe Alicia would be able to pet her....

The kitten stared at the sandwich. The two pieces she'd already eaten had been so delicious. But now the rest of the sandwich was closer to the girl, and she wasn't sure that she was brave enough to go and take it.

But the smell.... She could still taste it in her mouth, and she was really hungry. She hadn't eaten in such a long time. After she had scrambled over the fence the afternoon before, she had run and climbed and run again, frightened and desperate to get away. Her cozy den in the box had suddenly been snatched from her and she didn't understand. She just knew that she wasn't safe there anymore.

She had only stopped in the big yard because she was tired. Wriggling through the tiny gap under the back fence had worn her out. She had simply lain down in the dry, shadowy space under the bush and gone to sleep. When she'd woken, it had been dark, and she had been so hungry. She'd finally understood that everything was different now. Her mother wasn't there to bring her food, and there was no one there to curl up and sleep with. She was lost and all alone.

She had been on her own before, of course. But she had always known that her mother would come back. The kitten would purr throatily, and her mother would wash her, licking her fur lovingly all over.

Now her fur was dusty and matted with dirt, and a clump of it had torn out when she had squeezed under the fence. She had sat there below the bush and tried to wash herself, but it wasn't the same and it only made her feel more lonely.

The night sounds seemed louder than they'd ever been before. Cars roared past and made her shudder with fright, and people laughed and shouted. Another cat had stalked through the yard, late at night, but it hadn't been her mother. She had jumped up eagerly, ready to run and nuzzle it, but all it had done was stare at her and she'd seen it fluff out its tail. Then it had walked along the side of the house, and the kitten had ducked back under the bush, knowing that she was more lost than ever.

As Alicia pursed her lips and tried to call to the kitten using sounds that she thought she would like, the kitten stared back at her and wondered what to do. The girl seemed quiet and gentle, not like those stomping men who had chased her away from her home. And she had food. Right now, food seemed to be the most important thing of all.

Slowly, paw by paw, the kitten came out of her hiding place and crept toward Alicia.

Chapter Five

"Alicia...."

"*Shhh!*"

"Alicia, is that a kitten? Is that the kitten from near the bakery?"

"Yes, but *shhh!* Please don't make her run away. She's really shy, Will. Come and sit down."

Will sat down, as slowly and quietly as he could, and stared at the kitten.

She stared back for a moment, but she was so busy devouring the rest of the chicken sandwich that she didn't really have time to worry about him.

"How did she get here?"

"I don't know." Alicia reached out one hand and held it by the plate, close enough for the kitten to sniff. The kitten glared at her and then butted gently at Alicia's hand.

Will giggled. "She's telling you to get off her sandwich."

"Maybe. Or she might be putting her scent on me," said Alicia. "That's what a cat's doing when it rubs its face against you. They've got scent glands there. They're saying we belong to them."

I want to belong to you, she added silently. *Please stay. Please, please, please.*

"Alicia," Will whispered. "Do you think—do you think she could be our cat? Can we keep her?" He looked around the yard. "We could make her a bed in the greenhouse. Wow, she actually finished all of that sandwich. Do you think she wants another one? Grandma asked if I wanted a sandwich but I said no. I could go and say that I've changed my mind...."

Alicia looked worried. "I don't like

telling Grandma lies—but we can't tell her the truth, can we? Dad said she wouldn't want a pet in the house. And this kitten really needs food. She's so skinny."

"The greenhouse isn't in the house!" Will said with a grin. "So we could just forget to tell her, it doesn't matter."

Alicia couldn't help thinking that it did matter, and that they were just twisting things around to be the way they wanted—but she wouldn't be able to handle it if Grandma made them take the kitten back to the alley. The greenhouse would be like a palace to a kitten who was used to living in a box. And Grandma didn't usually go down to the far end of the yard. It would be all right.

And if she really had a kitten, she wouldn't be lying to Sarah anymore.

"Yes." She nodded. "Go and ask Grandma if you can have a sandwich. With lots of chicken."

"Oh, dear, what's the matter with that poor little girl?" Grandma sped up as they made their way home from school. She hurried down the pavement toward a toddler standing outside the bakery next to a little scooter and howling. "I hope she's not lost."

"She isn't, Grandma. Look, I can see her mom coming." Alicia pointed to a lady running toward the little girl.

"Good." Grandma bent over the little

girl. "What happened, sweetheart? Did you fall off your scooter?"

The little girl stared back at her and shook her head. She stopped crying.

Grandma smiled at the little girl's mother, who had reached them at last and was now crouched next to her daughter, hugging her and all out of breath. "I'm sorry," Grandma began. "We didn't see what happened, but she says she didn't fall."

"Mommy! The cat!" And the little girl began to howl again.

"Oh, Megan! Did you try and pet a cat? Did he scratch you?"

The little girl nodded and wailed louder, holding up her arm toward her mom.

Alicia sucked in her breath through

her teeth—Megan had a long scratch down the inside of her arm. It wasn't bleeding very much, but it obviously hurt.

"Some cats are just grumpy, Megan. You know I said not to chase them." Her mom sighed. "Don't worry, baby. We'll go home and put some medicine on it."

Alicia bit her lip. It probably wasn't the right time to say that the cat must have been scared if the little girl had tried to grab it.

"It was probably that stray tabby that lives down at the end of the alley," Grandma said. "Stray cats can be very wild and fierce."

Alicia and Will exchanged glances, thinking of the little black-and-white kitten, curled up in the greenhouse back at home. They'd made her a cozy bed out of one of the cardboard boxes they'd had for packing up their things, tipped on its side and lined with an old sweatshirt of Alicia's. Then they'd put out a trail of chicken sandwich pieces to show the kitten where the greenhouse was.

Alicia and Will had done their best to make it into the nicest den a kitten could have. They'd even made her a litter box out of an old seed tray they'd found on one of the greenhouse shelves—it had been full of dusty earth. Alicia had a feeling the kitten might not know what it was for, since she was a stray and was used to going to the bathroom anywhere, but if she was going to be an indoor cat one day, it was important to try. Will had brought her a small saucer full of water from the outside faucet, too.

That morning, before they went to school, Alicia had snuck outside with some cereal and milk. It wasn't the best thing for a kitten, she knew, but they didn't have any cat food. Anyway, the kitten hadn't seemed to mind. She had buried her face in it eagerly and when Alicia finally had to go, the kitten had been blissfully licking milky bits off her whiskers.

She hadn't looked very wild and fierce at all. She was still shy, of course. But when Alicia had arrived with the bowl, she hadn't run away, or hidden herself behind the wobbly towers of flowerpots. Instead, she'd just pricked her ears, wary, but hopeful.

Alicia and Will lagged behind Grandma for the rest of the way home. "Did you hear what Grandma said about stray cats being fierce?" Will asked anxiously.

Alicia nodded. "I know. I was really wishing we could tell her about Catkin."

"Catkin?" Will blinked in surprise. "You named her?" He frowned a little. Alicia could tell he was hurt that she'd given the kitten a name without talking to him.

"Grandma used to have a black-and-white cat named Catkin," Alicia explained. "She was telling me about her. It's a really sweet name and I thought that maybe if we called the kitten Catkin, too, it would remind her of it. But now Grandma's thinking about mean, fierce cats instead. It's the worst timing ever."

"Ohhh." Will nodded. "I see. But our

Catkin's sweet, Alicia. She's not fierce at all. Grandma will see that, won't she?"

"I think so. But let's not tell her just yet that we've got Catkin in the greenhouse. She'll have to go on being our secret kitten. And don't tell Dad, either!"

"Come on, you two!" Grandma called back. "It's starting to rain."

Alicia and Will sped up, the first fat drops splashing onto the pavement as they dashed after Grandma.

"What if she gets wet?" Will hissed. "The greenhouse has all those big holes in the roof! She'll get wet for sure!"

"You're right," Alicia muttered back. She smiled at Will. "You know that big old wardrobe in my bedroom…. Maybe we could hide her in there."

"Why not in my bedroom?" Will said.

"Because you don't have a wardrobe, just drawers. And because your bedroom is next to Dad's! Mine's up those creaky stairs, and I can always hear people coming. So I've got time to hide a kitten in my wardrobe before they get to the top, you see?"

"I guess so." Will sighed heavily.

Alicia smiled to herself, imagining falling asleep tonight with the faint sound of purring echoing out from her wardrobe. Or maybe even a small furry ball of kitten on the end of her bed. "I hope she understands we're trying to help," Alicia said suddenly. "She might not want to come inside. She's probably never been in a house before." Alicia had thought they'd be able to tempt Catkin inside gradually. She'd never thought of doing it so soon.

Will grinned at her. "I think if you gave her a chicken sandwich she'd probably go anywhere!"

Chapter Six

"Distract Grandma! Show her your cut knee," Alicia muttered, thinking of Megan and her scratch. She had the wet kitten and her old sweatshirt bundled up in her arms, and there was a lot of squeaking and wriggling going on. She'd taken the cheese from her lunch box (she'd saved it on purpose) and they'd snuck outside while

Grandma was taking off her coat and changing into her slippers. Catkin had been so excited about the cheese that she'd hardly minded when Alicia had picked her up. But now Alicia needed to get upstairs quickly. "Go in the bathroom…. Pretend you're looking for the first-aid box. Quick!" The armful of sweatshirt was wriggling like mad. "It's all right, Catkin. Just a tiny bit longer."

Will ran in through the back door and then into the bathroom. If he could get Grandma to follow him in there, she wouldn't see Alicia dash past.

"Grandma! My knee's bleeding! Can you get me a bandage? I fell down at school."

Alicia could hear Grandma bustling through the kitchen and then the squeak of the bathroom door. It was on Dad's DIY list to oil that door, so she was glad he hadn't done it yet. Huddling Catkin close, she darted through the kitchen, into the hallway and up the stairs.

Up in her room, she kicked the door gently shut and put her bundle down on the floor. Catkin shook her way out of the sweatshirt looking indignant and hissed faintly at Alicia.

"I'm sorry," Alicia whispered back. "I couldn't let Grandma see you. And it's really pouring out there now. I bet your box is soggy already. I'll make you a new bed. Look."

She grabbed another cardboard box off the teetering pile in the corner of her room and put it sideways in the bottom of her wardrobe, shoving all her shoes to one side. Catkin was still standing on the sweatshirt, so Alicia made a nest shape out of her woolly winter scarf and put that in the box instead. Then she put the last piece of cheese down in front of the box, too. It was still sitting in one of Grandma's little plastic containers, which made a perfect cat-food bowl.

"I'll get you some water in a minute," Alicia promised. "And the litter box. Your things are just outside the back door. Will brought them in from the greenhouse."

She looked at the kitten home thoughtfully and then at Catkin, who had slunk under her bed. The kitten looked worried.

"I know it's strange," Alicia told her quietly. "But we're nice. Really. And there's more cheese." She tapped her fingernails against the wardrobe door to make Catkin look and then tipped up the plastic container to show her. "Did you want another chicken sandwich instead? Are they your favorite? They're my favorite, too."

Catkin edged out from under the bed, sniffing. She was confused. But she had never had so much food before—her brother and sister had always fought for more of their mother's milk and the same with the scraps. It wasn't just the sandwiches and the cereal or the cheese, either—the two children had been so gentle. Alicia and Will had whispered to her and tried to purr at her, and that morning Alicia had run one finger softly all down her back, which had tickled. It had been strange and different, but she had liked it. And now there was another soft box bed and more food. She liked being inside, all warm and dry. So she padded cautiously across the room and stopped to sniff at Alicia's fingers. Then she butted her head up against Alicia's hand and went to nibble daintily at the cheese in the container.

Alicia sat watching her, smiling to herself. Her own kitten. In her own bedroom. Almost, anyway.

Then she froze. The steps up to her room were creaking. She was just sitting forward, ready to scoop Catkin further into the wardrobe and close the door, when she heard Will hissing, "It's only me! I've got the litter box!"

Alicia wriggled back slowly and went to open the door. "Wow! How did you do that?"

"Grandma's on the phone with Aunt Susie. She'll be a while. Angel Katie did really well at her ballet performance." Angel Katie was what they called their perfect little cousin. "Grandma was in the living room and she didn't see me at all. I've got the water, too."

"That's great. If I move my shoes and put them under my desk instead, we can put the litter box in the corner of the wardrobe. And this newspaper I used to wrap my photo frames can go underneath, just in case. Don't worry, Catkin. We're just making it nice for you."

"I hope she understands what to do," Will said doubtfully. "What if she pees in the wrong place? Like, I don't know, in your slippers?"

Alicia grinned at him. "Yuck. But actually, I don't think I'd mind. She's only little. I remember when you were a baby and you peed in Dad's face when he was changing your diaper."

Will turned red. "No, you don't! You can't remember that. You were little yourself."

"Well, I remember Dad telling me about it once, anyway. I bet Catkin won't make as much mess as a baby."

Catkin finished the cheese and sniffed thoughtfully at the litter box. Then she snuggled up on Alicia's scarf and pulled the sweater over herself, almost like a blanket. She tucked her nose comfortably under her tail, and as the two children watched, she fell fast asleep.

"I hope Grandma didn't go into your room for anything today," Will whispered to Alicia as they hurried across the playground the next afternoon. It was Friday, and everyone was running and swinging their bags, eager to get home and start the weekend.

"Me, too. But I don't think she would have. I took all of my dirty clothes downstairs and put them in the washing machine for her. And Dad vacuumed my room a couple of days ago. Catkin was really good last night. She didn't meow or anything, and she even used the litter box. This morning she was sitting on my windowsill when I woke up, just looking out the window." Alicia crossed her fingers. "Look, there's Grandma by the gate. She doesn't look angry, does she? Not like someone who's found a kitten in a wardrobe." They waved to Grandma and she waved back, smiling.

Just then someone called out her name. "Alicia!" It was Sarah.

Alicia swung around and beamed at her friend. "Hello!"

"Alicia, can I ask you a big favor?" Sarah said pleadingly, as they walked toward the gate. "I live near you, you know. Just a couple of streets down. Do you think I could stop by your house for five minutes on the way home? Just to see your kitten? Pleeease? My mom said it was fine if you said I could."

Alicia stopped walking and swallowed hard. She really wanted to say yes.

Maybe she could even tell Sarah the secret. But there wasn't time. Grandma would hear them, because she was really close. In fact, she was coming toward them, smiling. She was probably about to invite Sarah to come over and play.

"I-I can't today…," Alicia whispered, her eyes darting sideways at Grandma. "I've got—dance class." Grandma had been talking about signing her up for dance classes—there were some at the church hall, not far away. It was the first thing that came into her head.

It was a shame that Will blurted out, "I've got to go to soccer!" at the same time.

"We've got both," Alicia said hurriedly. "Friday just isn't a good day."

Grandma was standing next to them

now, looking curious, and Alicia could see Sarah's mom coming over, too.

"If you don't want me to come—" Sarah started to say, sounding a little hurt.

"It isn't that! I do want you to, I really do!"

"You just had to say no—I thought we were friends!"

"We are!" Alicia said anxiously. "It's just—not today. Another day!"

Sarah nodded, but she still looked really disappointed. She grabbed her mom's hand and pulled her away down the street, leaving Alicia and Will and Grandma staring at each other in confusion.

"Alicia, what's the matter? Wasn't that Sarah, the nice girl who lives on Timber Trail? Did you have a fight with her?"

"Yes." Alicia sniffed. "She wanted to come to our house."

"Well, why didn't you let her? She could have had dinner with us."

"It wasn't that. I can't explain. Please can we go home?" Alicia reached out and took Grandma's hand. "Please."

"All right." But Grandma still sounded worried, and she held on to

Alicia's hand as they walked. Alicia could tell she hadn't finished asking about what had happened. "Alicia, was Sarah asking about a kitten?" she said at last as they walked past the alley. "I thought I heard her say something about visiting a kitten…."

Alicia swallowed. "But we don't have a kitten," she pointed out, trying to sound cheerful.

"Alicia…." Grandma pulled her hand gently to make her stop. "Go on ahead for a minute, Will. Here, you can take my keys. Go and open the front door. We'll follow you." She watched as Will walked on ahead and then she followed, walking along slowly with Alicia's hand held tight in hers. "Alicia, did you tell Sarah you had a kitten?"

Alicia didn't say anything. How could she explain?

Grandma went on thoughtfully. "Sometimes it's hard, when you really want to make friends—you make up stories. Little stories to make yourself sound more interesting. Everyone does it sometimes, Alicia. It's all right."

Alicia gaped up at her. "How did you know?"

"Like I said, everyone does it. But almost everyone gets caught, too, sweetie. You're going to have to explain to Sarah and say you're sorry, you know."

Alicia kicked at the pavement with her foot. "I know," she muttered. But inside she was saying, *I didn't make it up. It wasn't a lie. Well, it was when I first said it. But now I'm lying to you instead.... I wish we had told you about Catkin in the first place. What am I going to do?*

"Are you that desperate for a kitten?" Grandma asked suddenly.

Alicia blinked, shocked out of her worries. "Um. I would love one. But Dad said you didn't like pets. Because they were dirty."

Grandma sniffed. "Well, I do like everything to be clean," she agreed. "But a little cat.... Maybe we could think about it."

Alicia swallowed hard and tried to smile. Somehow she had to explain to Grandma that they had a little cat already....

When they got back to the house, Grandma made hot chocolate, and she even put marshmallows on the top as a treat. She let Alicia and Will take it upstairs, although she did say they had to be careful not to spill any.

"Dinner will be ready in about an hour," she reminded them. "Your dad's working late tonight, so we're not waiting for him today."

Alicia and Will carried the hot chocolate upstairs to Alicia's room, with the sandwiches they'd both saved from lunch. At the top of the steps, outside the door, they stopped and looked at each other worriedly. Somehow Alicia felt convinced that the kitten wouldn't be there. Maybe they had imagined it all. She reached out and turned the handle, peering cautiously around the door.

Over in the wardrobe, the kitten lifted her head and yawned. Then she looked up at them and nosed at the empty bowl, clearly hoping for some food.

"Hello," Alicia whispered, starting to shred up her sandwich. "Did you miss us?"

Catkin yawned again and, very faintly, Alicia heard her purr.

"You're happy to see us! You're actually purring. Oh, Catkin. If only we could show you to Grandma right now. I'm sure she'd want to keep you." She patted Catkin's head, loving the feeling of the silky fur under her fingers. "This weekend, somehow, we'll find a way to tell her. We have to."

Chapter Seven

When Alicia and Will's dad got home late that night, he sat across the kitchen table from their grandma, eating his dinner.

"What's the matter?" he asked, as he wiped a bit of bread around his plate to mop up the gravy. "You've hardly said anything since I got home, Mom."

Grandma sighed and put down her cup of tea. "I'm just a little worried about Alicia. I'm not sure she's settling in all that well with the other girls at school. She had an argument with one of them this afternoon just as I was picking her up. She didn't want to talk about it very much, but it seems as though she'd told this girl—Sarah is her name—that we had a kitten."

Dad stared at her. "But why on earth would she say that?"

Grandma shrugged. "To fit in? To make herself sound more exciting? We're asking a lot of them, you know, starting at a new school."

Dad's shoulders slumped. "I guess so. But I thought it was the best thing to do...."

"I still think it is." Grandma reached over and patted his hand. "But I'm wondering if a pet would help Alicia settle in better."

"You don't like pets!"

"What gave you that idea? I wouldn't want a dog—I couldn't manage the walking—but I love cats!" Grandma smiled at him, a little sadly. "Actually, I suppose we didn't have any pets when you were younger, did we? I haven't had a cat of my own for a long time.

Not since Catkin died. She was 20, and I'd had her since I was a little girl. I didn't want another cat for a while after that, and somehow then it just never seemed to be the right time. But I wouldn't mind a cat now. Especially with Alicia and Will to help take care of it."

"Well, it would be wonderful for Alicia," Dad agreed. "I always said no before, because we were out of the house all the time." He got up and took his plate over to the dishwasher. "I'll go and check on her. I know she'll probably be asleep, but I just want to make sure that she's all right…."

Catkin woke up as the morning light shone into Alicia's room. She didn't have any blinds on the windows yet, and the morning was bright and sunny. The kitten stretched blissfully, padding her paws into a patch of sun just outside the wardrobe. Then she hunched up the other way, arching her back, and stepped delicately out into Alicia's bedroom.

Alicia was still fast asleep, huddled up under her comforter, so Catkin jumped up onto the bed to sniff at her. She smelled interesting, like breakfast and warm sunshine. But she didn't wake up when Catkin dabbed a chilly nose against her ear—only muttered and turned over, which made the comforter shift alarmingly. Catkin jumped down before she slid off and sat on the rug.

When she'd washed her ears thoroughly, both sides, Catkin stalked off across the room. Something was different, and she hadn't quite figured out what it was. There was something in the air, something fresh and new.

The door was open!

Alicia had shut it carefully, of course, when she came upstairs to go to bed.

But then her dad had come up to check on her. Catkin and Alicia had both been fast asleep, and neither of them had seen that he had left the door ajar. Just wide enough for a small, determined paw to hook it open.

Catkin nosed her way out and started to hop carefully—front feet, then back feet—down the stairs. It felt unfamiliar. Then she trotted along the landing, sniffing curiously at the different doors. She padded into Will's room, but a wobbly pile of books slid over when she nudged it, so she darted out again and set off down the next flight of stairs to the bottom. She sniffed her way carefully down the hallway and into the kitchen.

Most of the food was put away in

cupboards, but Dad had left a loaf of bread out on the counter, and Catkin could smell it. She sat on the floor, staring up and thinking….

Alicia woke up when the sunny patch from the window moved around onto her bed. She blinked sleepily, wondering why it was that she felt so happy and scared all at the same time. Then she sat up straight, remembering.

Catkin!

Today they *had* to find a way to tell Grandma and Dad what had happened, and make them see that Catkin needed to stay with them.

The kitten wasn't sitting on the

windowsill the way she had been the day before, so Alicia kneeled up in bed and leaned over to peer into the wardrobe. "Catkin," she called. "Here, little kitten!"

But no little kitten face appeared, and Alicia's heart began to beat faster. "Where did you go?" she muttered. She hopped out of bed and crouched down to check underneath, but there was nothing there except dust. No Catkin hiding in the cardboard boxes, or behind the little bookshelf by the door.

The open door.

Alicia gasped. "I shut it!" she whispered to herself. "I know I did. Oh, no." She hurried down the stairs, going as fast as she could on tiptoe, so she wouldn't wake Dad or Grandma. She dashed into Will's room.

"Wake up! Will, wake up! Have you seen Catkin? I don't know where she is."

Will stared at her sleepily, blinking like an owl, and then he squeaked and jumped out of bed.

"Where would she go?"

"Shhh! I don't know, maybe the kitchen?"

Will nodded. "Definitely the kitchen."

They hurried down the stairs, freezing every time one of them creaked. The house was old and they hadn't had time to learn which stairs to step over.

"Dad will hear us," Alicia whispered miserably. "We have to find her and get her back into my room." She kneeled down on the kitchen floor, looking around. She hadn't noticed how many tiny, kitten-sized hiding places there were in here before. On the chairs, under the table. Down the side of the oven. "Oh! What if she climbed into the washing machine?" Alicia gasped. "I read about a cat who did that once."

But the washing machine was empty, and so were all the other spots they could think of. Alicia sat down on the floor, looking helpless. "I can't think of anywhere else," she said. "All the windows are closed, aren't they?"

Will nodded. "It was cold last night. Unless—Grandma always sleeps with her bedroom window open."

A large tear spilled down the side of Alicia's nose. "Maybe she went out that way, then. She didn't want to stay. Catkin's gone!"

Chapter Eight

"What's the matter with you two? Why are you up at seven o'clock on a Saturday morning?" Grandma demanded. She was standing in the kitchen doorway, wrapped in her robe. "Alicia, you're crying! What's wrong?" She put her arms around Alicia, pulling her up from the floor.

"We've lost her!" Alicia sobbed into

Grandma's shoulder. She didn't care about keeping Catkin a secret anymore. It was too late now.

"Lost who?" Grandma stared at Alicia, puzzled, and so did Dad, who'd come in behind her, looking sleepy.

"Catkin," Will explained, coming to lean against Dad's robe. "Our kitten. Alicia found her in the yard. She was in Alicia's wardrobe, but when we woke up she was gone."

"You had a kitten shut in your wardrobe?" Dad said slowly.

"Not shut in," Alicia shook her head, gulping back tears. "Just her bed was in there and her litter box. She could go anywhere in my room. We couldn't leave her in the greenhouse—the glass is full of holes and it was pouring on Thursday night."

Dad and Grandma looked shocked. "But what were you feeding her?" Grandma asked, frowning.

"Sandwiches, mostly. She loves chicken." Alicia sniffed. "Just like me. We saved some of our lunches for her and she was getting tame. We thought she was going to stay with us, but now she's run away. She must have gone through your window, Grandma. It's the only one that was open." Alicia slumped down on one of the kitchen chairs.

Grandma moved slowly over to the counter to put the kettle on, wiping away the breadcrumbs and pushing shut a half-open drawer on the way. "I need a cup of tea," she said. "A kitten in your wardrobe...."

"Where did she come from in the first place? That's what I want to know," Dad said, sitting down across from Alicia with Will on his knee.

"The alley down by the bakery," Alicia explained tiredly. "There were three of them—the two tabbies got adopted, but nobody cared about the little black-and-white kitten. And then she just turned up in our yard."

"And you named her Catkin? Like my Catkin?" Grandma asked, getting mugs out of the cupboard.

"You said your kitten was black-and-white, too," Alicia explained. "And it's a sweet name. It was just right."

"Oh, dear," Grandma sighed. "Maybe she was just too wild to be a pet, Alicia. If she's never really known people...."

"But she wasn't wild," Alicia tried to explain. She could feel herself starting to cry again. "She was shy, but she purred at us. And she loved our food, even if she didn't really love us yet."

"Well, maybe we could go back to the alley by the shops and look for her," Grandma said thoughtfully, leaning over to get a clean dish towel out of the drawer.

"You mean—if we found her, we could bring her back home again?" Alicia gasped. "We can keep her?" She jumped up. "Can we go over there now?"

Will wriggled off Dad's knee. "Right now?"

But Grandma was standing staring into the dish towel drawer. "I don't think we need to…. Look."

Alicia leaned over and clapped her hand across her mouth. Curled up among Grandma's neatly stacked dish towels was a black-and-white kitten, half-asleep and blinking up at them in confusion.

"I shut the drawer…," Grandma said. "When I went to make the tea. It was open, just a little. You know how that drawer sticks sometimes…."

"Just enough for a skinny kitten to climb in, but not enough for us to see her!" Alicia said, her eyes wide.

Sleepily, Catkin stared up at Alicia and Grandma and let out a little purr. Maybe there was going to be food. The bread seemed like a long time ago, and it had been a lot of effort to get up onto the counter and steal a slice. She was hungry again.

"What a sweetheart," Grandma said, laughing as Catkin stepped carefully out of her nest in the drawer. She rubbed her furry face against Grandma's hand and purred even louder. "Just like my Catkin," Grandma said, petting her ears. "You're staying now, aren't you?"

Catkin jumped down to the floor and wove her way around Grandma's ankles and then Alicia's, still purring.

"That means yes," Alicia whispered. "I know it does."

"You actually had her hidden in your wardrobe?" Sarah asked Alicia again, as they followed Grandma home from school on Monday afternoon. "You had a secret kitten?"

"Yes. And I really wanted you to see her, but I couldn't let Grandma find out. Or I thought I couldn't. It turns out we probably should have just told her to start with."

"That wouldn't have been as exciting," Sarah said, shaking her head.

"No." Alicia smiled at her. "It *was* wonderful, Catkin being our secret. But now we can play with her without worrying about Dad and Grandma. And she still likes my bedroom best in all of the house."

"Should we stop and buy some cupcakes, girls?" Grandma suggested as they reached the bakery. "Oh, Will, come back!"

Alicia and Sarah giggled as Will raced ahead, flinging open the door of the bakery. When they caught up with him, he was already telling Emma, who was behind the counter, that he wanted a marshmallow cream cupcake.

"You know the black-and-white

kitten, the one that was living in your yard?" Alicia said shyly to Emma, after they'd chosen their cupcakes. "She came into our yard, and we're going to keep her!"

Emma smiled delightedly. "Oh, that's such good news! I looked for her, after you two told me she was there, but I never saw her. I did wonder if you'd imagined her."

"No, she's just a little shy." Alicia smiled to herself, remembering Catkin running madly around the kitchen after a ping-pong ball that morning and then collapsing in her lap, exhausted, with her paws in the air. She wasn't shy with them, not anymore.

"I've got news for you, too," Emma went on, as she put their chocolate cupcakes into a bag. "I called the cat shelter about the kittens' mom, to ask them what the best thing was to do. They're going to catch her and spay her so she doesn't have more kittens. They said she probably won't ever be tame enough to be a housecat, but if she's not trying to feed kittens all the time she'll be a lot less thin and worried, poor thing. So they'll bring her back and she can live in the yard. We'll put scraps out for her."

"Thank you!" Alicia forgot to be shy and gave Emma a hug. "You're amazing. I never even thought of doing that!"

"Can we bring Catkin back to visit her?" Will asked, reaching into his bag and picking the sprinkles off his cupcake.

"Maybe." Alicia smiled, imagining the two cats nose to nose, sniffing hello. All of a sudden she couldn't wait to get home and see Catkin and show her to Sarah, too.

Her own kitten, not-so-secret anymore....

HOLLY WEBB

Holly Webb started out as a children's book editor, and wrote her first series for the publisher she worked for. She has been writing ever since, with more than 100 books to her name. Holly lives in England with her husband, three young sons, and several cats who are always nosing around when she is trying to type on her laptop.

For more information about Holly Webb visit:

www.holly-webb.com
www.tigertalesbooks.com